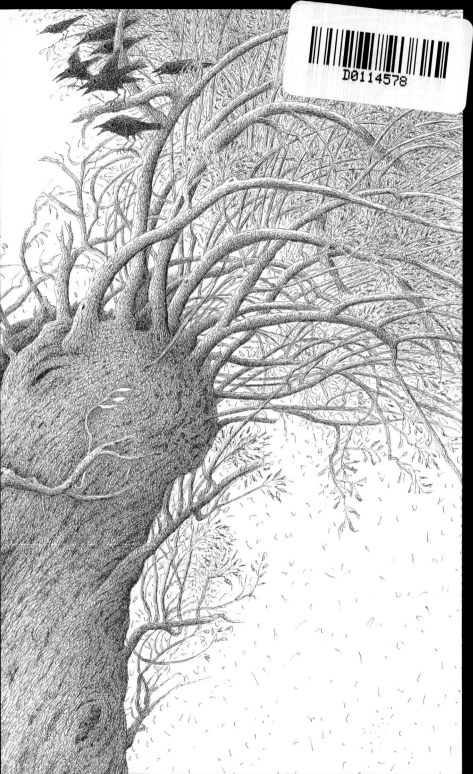

The Duck & the Owl

A CHILDREN'S STORY BY *Hannah Johansen*

ILLUSTRATED BY *Käthi Bhend*

Translated from the German by John S. Barrett

David R. Godine · Publisher · Boston

The Duck and the Owl

First U. S. edition published in 2005 by
David R. Godine, Publisher
Post Office Box 450
Jaffrey, New Hampshire 03452
www.godine.com

Originally published in Switzerland as
Die Ente und den Eule by Carl Hanser Verlag

Copyright © Nagel & Kimche im Carl Hanser Verlag
München Wien 1993
English translation copyright © 2005 by John S. Barrett

LIBRARY OF CONGRESS CATALOGING-IN-PUBLICATION DATA
Johansen, Hanna, 1939—
[Ente und die Eule. English]
The duck & the owl : a children's story / by Hannah Johansen ;
illustrated by Kathi Bhend ; translated from the German by
John S. Barrett.— 1st U. S. ed.
p. cm.
title: Duck and the owl.
Summary: A duck and an owl contemplate starting a
friendship, despite their differences in appearance and behavior.
ISBN-13: 978-1-56792-285-1 (hardcover : alk. paper)
ISBN-10: 1-56792-285-6 (hardcover : alk. paper)
[1. Ducks—Fiction. 2. Owls—Fiction. 3. Friendship—Fiction.]
I. Title: Duck and the owl. II. Bhend, Käthi, ill.
III. Barrett, John S. IV. Title.
PZ7.J617DU 2005
[E]—DC22
2005013235

First Edition, 2005
PRINTED IN CANADA

The Duck & the Owl

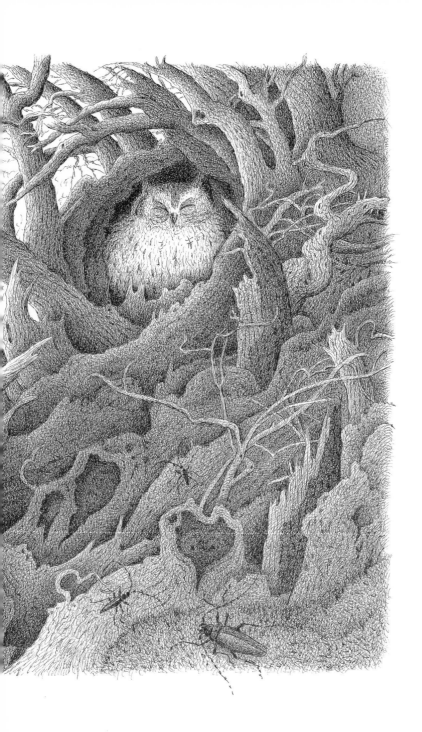

Once there was a birch tree

standing in a meadow.

And right next to the meadow
was a sparkling pond
with a duck swimming around
in the water.

Now and again
she would dip her beak in.

Then the duck climbed out,
shook herself,
and took a long look
up at the tree.

When she'd looked long enough,
she called out,

"Hey, you up there!"

"Hmmm," muttered a voice
way up in the birch tree.

3763370

"Are you a real owl?"
asked the duck.

"Hmmm."

"C'mon down,"
yelled the duck.

"Hmmm,"
muttered the owl,
and yawned.
Then he came
fluttering down.

"Oh," said the duck,
"I really didn't know
owls had
such beautiful, big wings."

"Hmmm," said the owl again,
(but he was happy
that the duck thought
his wings were beautiful.)

"Why are you always saying 'Hmmm'?
Can't you say anything else?"

"Of course I can,"
said the owl,
"but I don't feel like it.
I was just about to
go to sleep."

"Oh, my goodness,"
said the duck.
"How can you sleep
in broad daylight?
Nobody does that."

"I don't know
what you mean,"
said the owl.
"I always sleep during the day."

"That's funny,"
said the duck.
"You're supposed to
sleep at night."

"Supposed to sleep at night
you say?
No way!
It's much too exciting
to sleep at night
when it's really dark,
when you can open your eyes
really wide
and wait
for something good to eat
to come by."

"You must be a little funny in the head,"
said the duck.
"Things to eat don't come walking by.
You have to swim around
and dive down
and look and look
until you find something."

"That's a silly way to eat."
muttered the owl.

The duck got mad.
"It's not silly,
it's normal!"
she said angrily.

"You must be a little funny in the head,"
said the owl.
"The normal way
is to go through the woods
in the dark
v e e e r y quietly.

And then, when some little animal
makes a rustling noise
in the dry leaves . . .

. . .you dive down
quick as a wink
And eat it up."

"Oh yuck!"
screamed the duck.
"That's *horrible!*
Just thinking about it is
making me sick to my stomach."

"Well, what do you eat?"
replied the owl.
He was getting mad, too.
"You eat weeds
from the bottom of the pond?
Revolting!
The idea is making *me* sick.
And how can anyone eat
in the middle of the *day*, anyway?"

Now the duck
hissed angrily,
"If you really want to know
you're *supposed* to eat in the daytime.
Everybody does it that way."

"Oh, come on –
nobody does that,"
screeched the owl.
"You don't get good and hungry
until it gets dark."

"That's really dumb,"
cackled the duck.
"Really dumb,
really dumb,
really dumb!"

And so the two of them
sat in the meadow and quarreled.
The owl opened and closed

his beak a few times
as if he were thinking things over.
Then he shook himself.

"Listen, duck," said the owl,
"why are we
quarreling, anyway?
Do you remember
why
we got started?"

"Of course,"
said the duck,
"because you do everything
the wrong way,
that's why."

"That's not true at all,"
said the owl.
"I don't do things the wrong way,
I do them a *different* way,
and it works out fine.
I just do things
the way owls do."

"And I do things
the way ducks do.
You're right.
We shouldn't
be quarreling
about it."

"Well,"
thought the owl to himself,
"I actually like the duck.
She has an odd way of looking at things,
but we can still be friends,
can't we?"

"What funny feet you have!"
said the owl.

"They're not funny,"
answered the duck,
"they're practical.
For swimming."

"Maybe they're
good for swimming,"
allowed the owl,
"if you like to *swim*.
And if I look at them the right way
I even think
they're pretty."

"Really!"
whispered the duck.

Then the owl said,
"Come with me.
My legs are beginning
To hurt down here.
Let's make ourselves comfy
up in the birch tree."

"What did you say?"
asked the duck.

"Let's fly up there,"
said the owl
"It's more comfortable sitting in a tree."

The duck had
never sat in a tree
in her life,
but if it would make the owl happy,
she was willing to give it a try.
"If you think so,"
she said.

Together
they flew upward. . .

. . . and sat down on a branch
where they could look far out
over the countryside.

"You can see more from here,"
said the owl with satisfaction.

"Well yes, I'll admit that,"
muttered the duck.
She looked down on the meadow
and on the pond
shimmering in the sunlight.

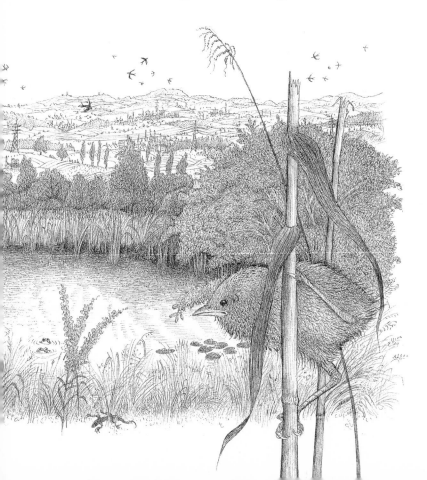

But she really wasn't happy at all,
sitting way up there
in a tree.
The whole time
she was afraid she'd fall down.

"I don't like it here,"
she said to the owl.
"Let's swim back and forth
in the water instead."

"Have you gone crazy?"
screeched the owl.
"In the *water?*
Are you trying to *kill* me?"

"Don't get so excited,"
said the duck.
"If you like,
we'll just sit down on the grass again.
You owls are probably too dumb
to be able to swim."

"And you ducks are so dumb
that you can't
even sit
in a tree."

"Oh my goodness,"
said the duck,
"here we are quarreling again."

"Because you *always* start it,"
said the owl.

"That's not true!"
yelled the duck angrily.
"I didn't start it,
you did!"

"No *you* did!" screamed the owl.

"No *you* did!" screamed the duck.

"No *you* did!" screamed the owl.

"Hey, why are you screaming like that?"
asked the duck.

"I'm not the one who's screaming,"
said the owl,
"*you* are."

"No, *you* are!"

"No, *you* are!"

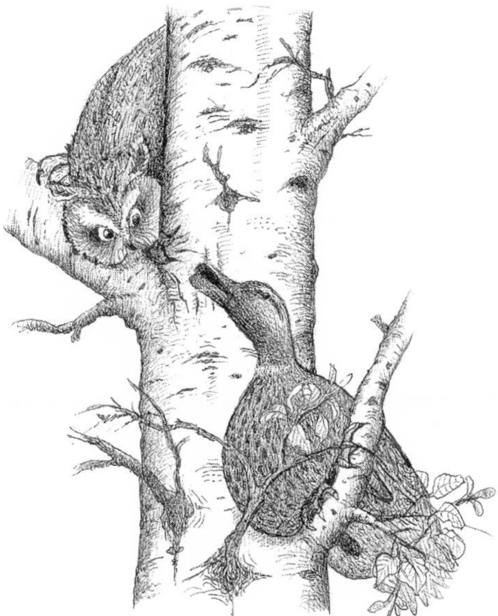

"No, *you* are!"

"Oh, my goodness,"
said the owl.
"I've had enough of this.
Why are we
always quarreling anyway?"

"Because you do everything
the wrong way."

"No, I don't," said the owl.
"You do!"

"No, you do," said the duck.

"No, you do," said the owl.

"No, you do," said the duck.

"But it doesn't matter,"
said the owl.
"We shouldn't be
quarreling about it."

The duck thought a moment
and said,
"No,
we shouldn't be.
But who starts it,
anyway?"

"You do, I think."

"You must be a little funny in the head,"
said the duck.
"You're the one who starts it."

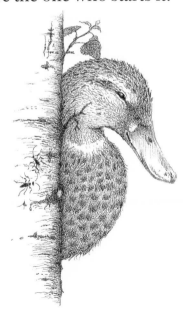

"Hmmm,"
said the owl.
"Sometimes I do start it.
But then you join right in."

"I do?"
screamed the duck.
She flapped her wings
in a huff.

"Don't make so much wind,"
said the owl.
"Do you want me to fall off?"

"Okay," said the duck,
"but if you want us to be friends,
you have to stop your screaming."

"You stop!"
said the owl.

"No, you!"

"No, you!"

"No, you!"

The the duck laughed
and said,
"I've had enough.
And besides, I'm hungry.
I get short-tempered when I'm hungry.
I'm going to look for
something to eat."

"And I'm tired.
I always get irritable
when I'm tired.
I think
I need a nap."

The duck flapped down
and landed on the pond.
Then she turned around,
looked up, and yelled,
"Goodbye for now, owl,
and sleep well."

"Hmmm,"
said the owl drowsily.
"You sleep well, too, duck."
His eyes were already
almost shut.

"Oh, right,"
he said then,
"you're not going to sleep.
You only sleep
when it gets dark.
Well, have a nice day, duck."

"See you again soon."

ABOUT THE AUTHOR

Born in Bremen in 1939, Hanna Johansen studied German literature, philology, and pedagogy at Marburg and Göttingen and in the United States. A resident of Zürich since 1972, she is the winner of the Swiss Children's Literature Prize and was a finalist for the Hans Christian Andersen Prize in 2000. She writes novels and stories for adults as well as for children, and in 2003 received the Solothurn Prize for her lifelong contribution to German-language literature.

ABOUT THE ILLUSTRATOR

Born in Olten, Switzerland, in 1942, artist Käthi Bhend studied graphic arts before working in advertising agencies in Lausanne and freelancing in Paris. Since the late 1970s, when she won a competition to illustrate Swiss schoolbooks, she has earned a reputation as the country's premier artist for children. Her children's books, many of which have been created in collaboration with Hanna Johansen, have received numerous awards, including the Swiss Children's Book Prize and the Premio Grafico of the Bologna Book Fair.

A NOTE ON THE TYPE

THE DUCK AND THE OWL *has been set in Bulmer, a type first cut in 1790 by William Martin for William Bulmer and Company's Shakspeare [sic] Printing Office, which was established during the reign of George III for the purpose of producing a new edition of Shakespeare's works. The type was revived with great success by ATF in 1928 and was soon made available for machine composition on the Monotype. While Bulmer draws from the tradition of Caslon, it is, like Baskerville, a transitional face, graced with characteristics that point toward the types cut some decades later by Giambattista Bodoni in Italy. More condensed than Baskerville, Bulmer reveals a debt to the Didot types in its increased contrast and refined serifs. Though it has been said that English printing suffered a general decline in the decades following Bulmer's death in 1830, the types that bear his name retained their luster to such a degree that no less a critic than Daniel Berkeley Updike would write, "They were very splendid of their kind."*

Design and composition by
Carl W. Scarbrough